READMOBILE
204 N Cascade, PO Box 717
Fergus Falls, MN 56538-0717

W9-DIR-328

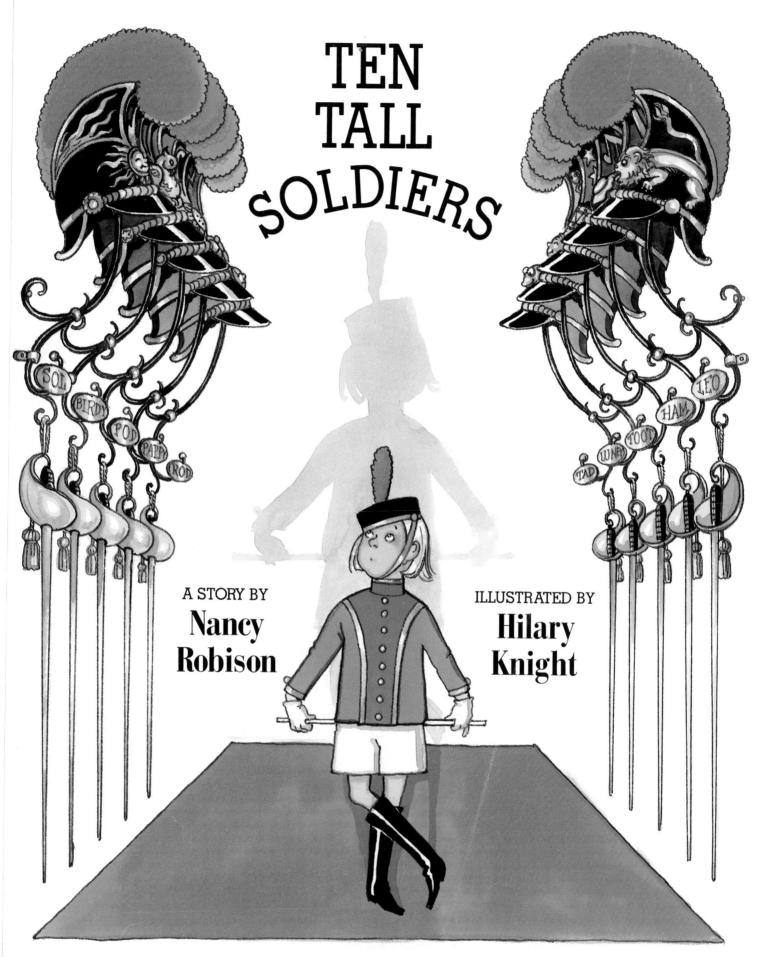

TEN
TALL
SOLDIERS

SOL BIRDY POD PATY ROD

TAD LUNK TOOT HAM LEO

A STORY BY
Nancy Robison

ILLUSTRATED BY
Hilary Knight

Aladdin Paperbacks
New York London Toronto Sydney Singapore

There once was a king who was short and round as a toadstool. He lived in a little stone castle and had ten tall soldiers who guarded him, for this little king was not very brave.

One cold night he stood by a glowing fire toasting himself to keep warm.

As he turned around, he saw a dreadful sight.

It was small and fierce looking. With warts. And horns. The king was terrified.

"GUARDS! GUARDS!" he shouted.

Ten tall soldiers dressed in blue with tall red hats came running. So did Peter.

The king trembled. "Help! Save me from the giant frog!"

The king watched as the frog grew more horns right before his eyes.

"Oh no!" he cried. "I can't look!"

The soldiers searched the room but they could not find the giant frog.

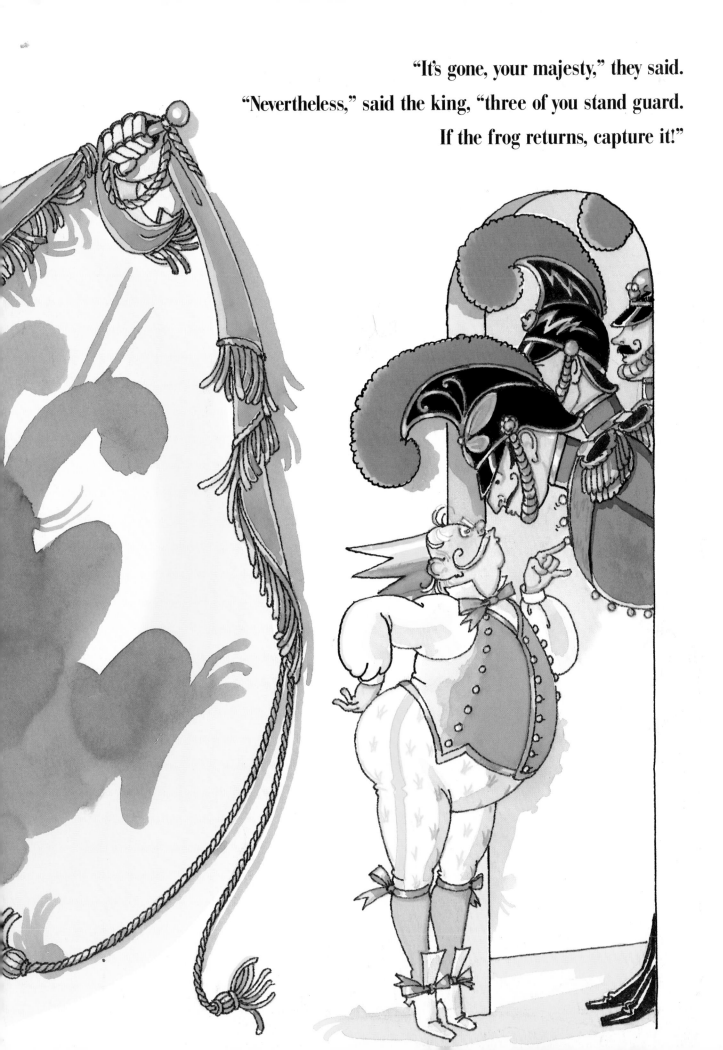

"It's gone, your majesty," they said.

"Nevertheless," said the king, "three of you stand guard.
If the frog returns, capture it!"

The next morning the king went to the kitchen to speak to the cook.
But the cook was not there. And no wonder. On the ceiling was another monster!
This one was fat and furry looking. With waving tentacles. The king was terrified.
"GUARDS! GUARDS!" he shouted.

Seven tall soldiers dressed in blue with tall red hats came running. So did Peter.

The king shivered in fear. "Help! Help! Save me from the giant jumping spider!"

The king watched as the spider grew bigger and more fierce looking than the frog.

"Oh no!" he cried. "I can't look!"

The soldiers searched the kitchen but they could not find the giant jumping spider.
"It's gone, your majesty," they said.

"Nevertheless," said the king,
"three of you stand guard.
If the spider returns, capture it!"

The king didn't know where to go to escape the scary creatures.
He tried the royal garden. Everything seemed peaceful and safe.

Until he turned around.

There, sneaking along the garden wall, was another monster!
This one was long and skinny. With a horned head and lizard legs.
The king was terrified.
"GUARDS! GUARDS!" he shouted.

Four tall soldiers dressed in blue with tall red hats came running.
So did Peter. The king shivered and shook all over. "Help! Help! Help!
Save me from the dreadful dragon!"

The king watched as the dragon grew many heads and many more legs.
It looked like a gigantic caterpillar.
"SLAY IT! SLAY THE DRAGON!" the king cried.

The soldiers searched and searched,
but they could not find the dragon.
"It's gone, your majesty," they said.

"Nevertheless," said the king,
"the rest of you stand guard
in the courtyard.
If the dragon returns, slay it!"

Peter stood alone.
He went to the king.
"You can come out now," he said.
"The dragon really is gone."

The king peeked out from his hiding place.
"Oh happy day!" he cheered,
and dashed toward the wall.
As he got near, a dark figure, short and
round as a toadstool, appeared.
"Guards! Guards!" the king whimpered.
"A new monster!"

The ten tall soldiers, standing guard elsewhere, did not hear the king's call.

But Peter stood at attention. "I don't see a monster," Peter said.

"There! Over there!" The king waved his arms wildly in the air.

"It won't hurt you," Peter said. "See? Watch!" He touched the wall.

"This is not a real monster." The king gasped.

The monster also waved its arms.

"Be gone with you! Shoo! Shoo!" whispered the king.

Carefully he reached out to touch the monster but only felt the wall.
Then the king began to laugh. "How silly of me! How very, very silly.
GUARDS! GUARDS!" he shouted.

Ten tall soldiers dressed in blue with tall red hats came running.

"There is no dragon here," the king said.

"None at all.

This is only my shadow!"

The king, the soldiers, and Peter all laughed.

Then the king said, "Peter, you are so brave,
you should be a soldier too."

"But I'm not very tall," said Peter.

"Tall or small, it doesn't matter," the king said.

"Bring him a coat and a tall red hat!"

From that day on,
every time the king saw his shadow,
he danced around in circles laughing.

And every time he called for his guards,
one short and ten tall soldiers dressed in blue came running.

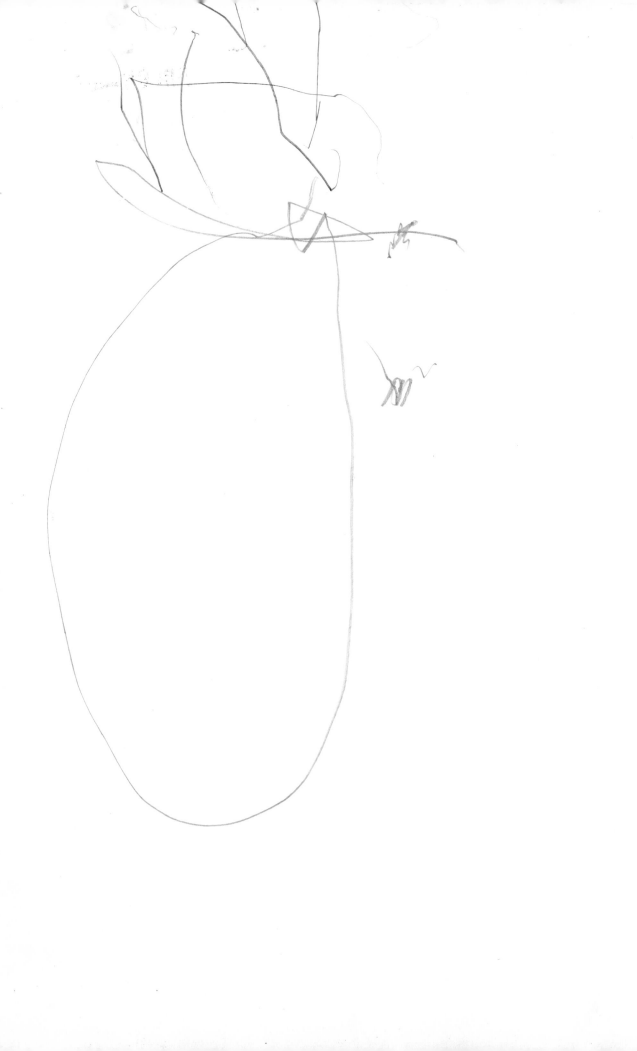